Santa Sees

Molly Nero

Illustrated by
Claire Nero

Halo
PUBLISHING
INTERNATIONAL

ISBN: 978-1-63765-068-4
LCCN: 2021912908

Halo Publishing International, LLC
www.halopublishing.com

Printed and bound in the United States of America

To Claire and Nick, who have always
kept my life filled with the magic
of watching you become you!

While sitting in my huge red chair on a cold, wintry night, I'm sipping on a steaming mug of hot chocolate thinking about children all around the world.

The roaring fire next to me warms my hands as I begin to read through a huge pile of papers on my big wooden desk. It is my "Naughty and Nice List."

Each page is filled with thousands of names. Some papers are already turned over because I have checked the names once and then checked them twice.

As I look over a new page, a name catches my eye. Taking a sip of cocoa, I hold the page up and smile. Right at the top, I see a very special name: your name.

You see, I DO know when you've been bad or good, but did you know my Christmas magic sees more of who you are each and every day? Everything you choose to do matters, and I want you to know why you are on my "Nice List."

I want you to know what I see.

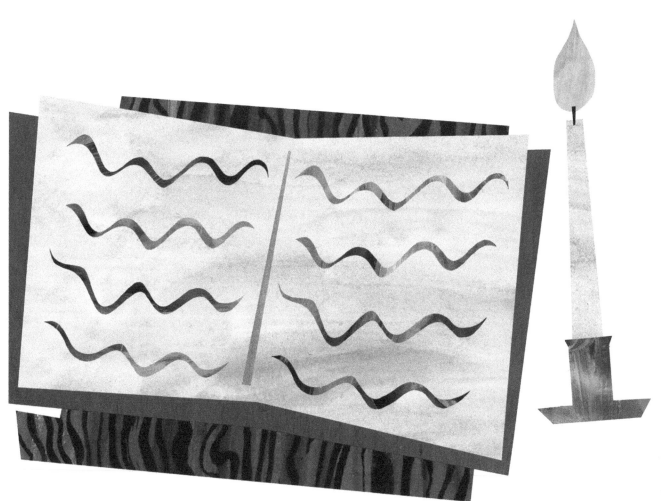

I see when you don't want to get out of bed early in the morning. It would be so nice to snuggle under the covers and keep on dreaming. But even when it is cold, you get out of bed and begin to get ready. Although you are sleepy, you try hard not to complain.

6

I see you make it to breakfast and not be late.

I see when you ask for something, and the answer is "No." You might feel frustrated, disappointed, or sometimes even mad.

no no non no no no no no no

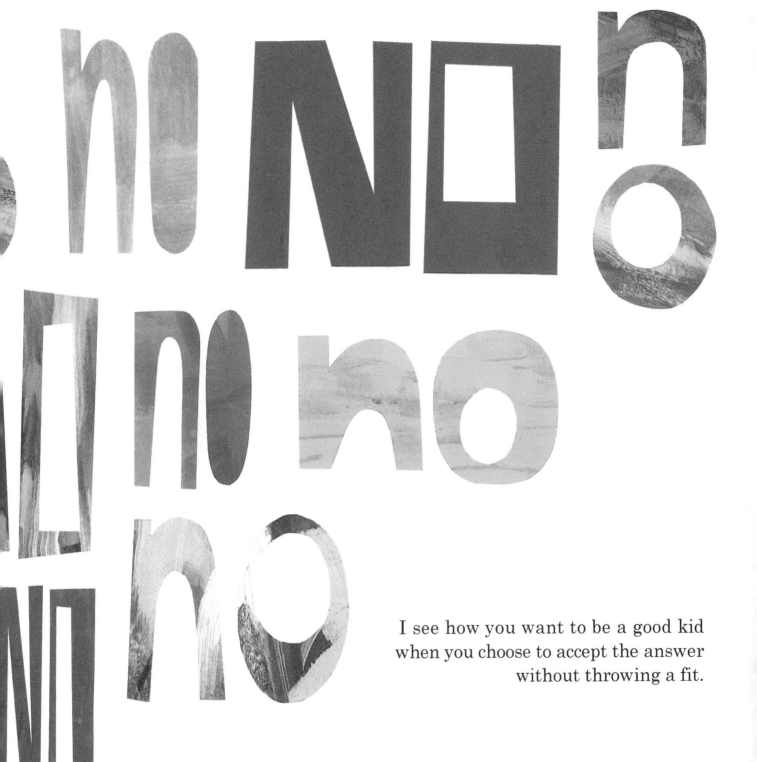

I see how you want to be a good kid when you choose to accept the answer without throwing a fit.

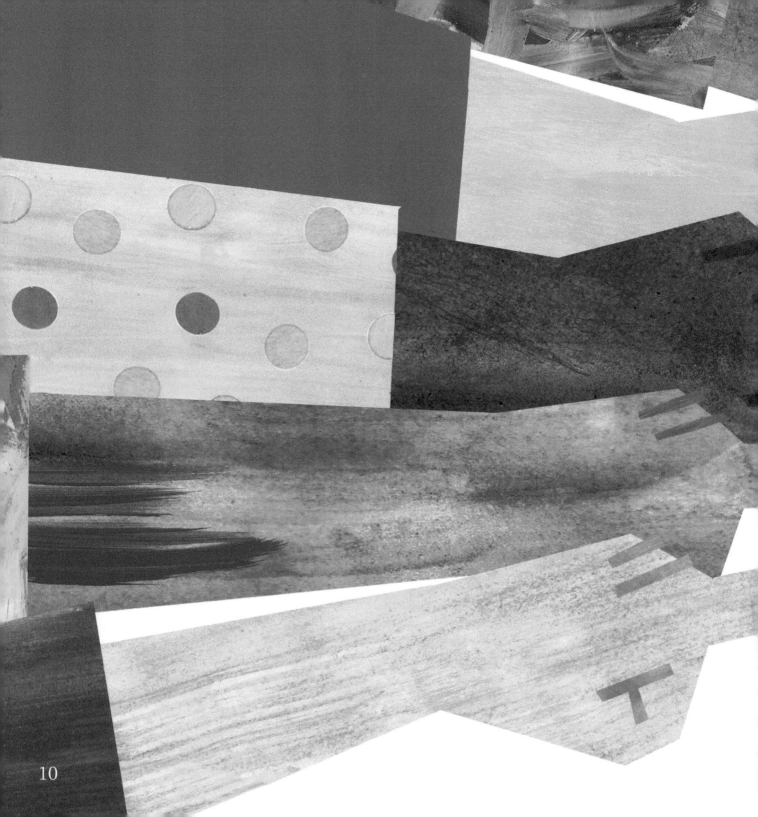

I see when kids say things to you that put them on the "Naughty List!" You choose not to act like that.

I see you take a breath, stay calm, and walk away.

I see you when you are asked to help around the house. I know you don't always want to quit playing or watching your favorite show, but you do.

I see you stop what you are doing to help.

I see you working hard as you learn new things. Sometimes it's fun. Other times it's very difficult, but you do your best to figure it out.

Even when you want to give up, I see you keep trying.

I see you laughing with your friends. You are happy to share and always play fair.

I see what a great friend you are.

I see you when your room is a mess with things all over the floor. You know you need to pick it up, and it seems like it will take forever.

You don't want to even start, but you do.

I see you take it one step at a time and get it all cleaned up.

please

I see you try to remember and use manners like saying "please" and "thank you." It's okay when you forget sometimes.

I see you always try to be grateful for what others do for you.

I see you smile at others, say "hello" to your neighbors, and help those around you. It makes a big difference in their lives. You are such a good person.

I see how kind you are to everyone.

It's caring, hard-working, giving kids that make me smile.

Kids who help others and know how to be a good friend.
You are one of those kids. You are good, for goodness sake!

That is what makes you so special.
That is why you are on my "NICE List." Thank you for being you!

Santa

About the Author

During years of teaching elementary students, Molly Nero desired to reach children beyond her classroom. Once her writing debut, *Smarty Pig*, became an award-winning book, it launched her vision to write stories that acknowledge and support kids. Today, a series of kid-friendly books are in development encouraging emergent readers with personalized stories. Kids can read about themselves going on adventures, problem-solving and being their best when sometimes faced with distractions and integrity challenges. Florida life keeps Molly's feet in the sand while her imagination dances on the waves!

About the Illustrator

Claire Nero is a character designer and illustrator based in Emeryville, CA. Proud daughter of the author, Claire was encouraged to pursue art as a career in her teenage years and has since worked for companies including Pixar Animation Studios, Disney TV, and Netflix. She is a vintage fashion collector and draws inspiration from the history each new piece has to offer. For inspiration, or when she is not creating and animating characters, Claire enjoys exploring her city, as well as other areas around the world. Claire's vision is to create a children's television program with the author, to continue the promotion of self-love and validation for children everywhere.

CPSIA information can be obtained
at www.ICGtesting.com
Printed in the USA
BVHW022339281121
622756BV00018B/625